RED FOX
ON THE MOVE

With all my love and thanks to David, Judith, Sasha,
Kevin, Keith, Luke, and Joe

First published in the United States
by Dial Books for Young Readers
A Division of Penguin Books USA Inc.
375 Hudson Street
New York, New York 10014

Published in Great Britain
by Frances Lincoln Limited
Copyright © 1992 by Hannah Giffard
All rights reserved
Printed in Hong Kong
First Edition
1 3 5 7 9 10 8 6 4 2

Library of Congress Cataloging in Publication Data
Giffard, Hannah.
Red Fox on the move / by Hannah Giffard.
p.   cm.
Summary: When they are moved out of their cozy den by an invading bulldozer,
Red Fox and his family find a new home in an unexpected place.
ISBN 0-8037-1057-7 (trade)
[1. Red fox—Fiction. 2. Foxes—Fiction.
3. Moving, Household—Fiction.] I. Title.
PZ7.G3627Rg 1992 [E]—dc20 90-25646 CIP AC

RED FOX
ON THE MOVE

◆ **Story and pictures by Hannah Giffard** ◆

Dial Books for Young Readers New York

Red Fox and Rose were sleeping peacefully in the den with their five young cubs—Boris, Poppy, Albert, Florence, and Pablo.

Suddenly the earth began to shake, and the giant teeth of a
bulldozer came crashing through the roof! The frightened foxes
sprang to their feet and scrambled out just in time.

Red Fox knew he would have to find his family a new home,
and he would have to find it soon. He led the way toward the woods.

But before the foxes could reach the trees, they had to cross the fast-flowing river.

Red Fox plunged into the icy cold water. The cubs hung back.
"Hold on to my tail!" he barked.

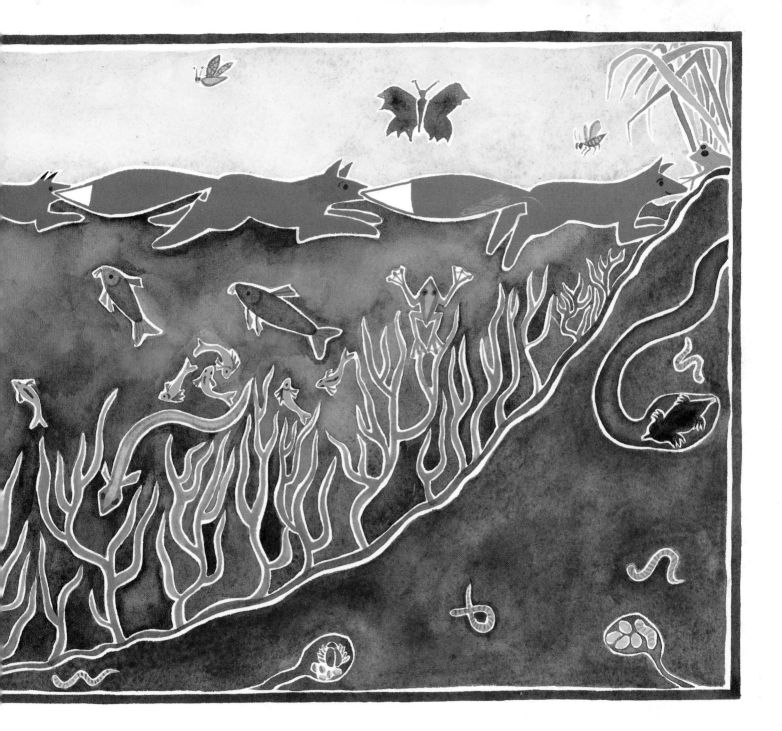

One by one they jumped in bravely behind Red Fox and Rose,
each cub holding on to the tail in front.

When they were safely across, Red Fox noticed a small hole in a sandbank. That looks like a perfect fox home, he thought.

Then an angry snake poked her head out.
"Stay away from my eggs," she hissed.

The foxes ran deeper into the woods.

"Look!" said Rose. "A perfect home, just like our old one."

It was a big hole in the base of an old, hollow oak tree.

Rose crawled inside and looked up. The large eyes of a furious owl looked down. "Go away!" he screeched. The foxes raced off.

"Look, everyone! I've found our new home!" shouted Pablo, the youngest and smallest of the cubs.

Then came a terrible squeal. Pablo had put his nose in a bees' nest!

"Run for your lives," cried Red Fox. And they did.

It was dusk. Tired and cold, the cubs started to whine.
Are there *any* fox homes left? Red Fox wondered desperately.
Then he spied a boat, and he had an idea.

"Follow me," said Red Fox.
They all jumped on board, curled up behind some boxes, and
went to sleep.

When the foxes woke up, they stared in shock. . . .
The boat was moving down the river.
"Where are we going?" whimpered the cubs.

They were heading for the city!
Red Fox knew he had made a terrible mistake.

By sunrise the boat arrived at the docks. "Stay away from the people," whispered Red Fox.

When Rose saw a railroad track, the foxes decided to follow it.

Red Fox and Rose led the cubs into a tunnel.
"Perhaps this will lead us out of the city," said Red Fox
hopefully.

Inside the tunnel was darker than night. Dripping water echoed all around them. And when at last they reached the other end, Pablo was gone—he had disappeared!

The foxes split up to search for him. "Pablo," they barked, "where are you?" But there was no reply. The unhappy foxes couldn't find him anywhere.

Suddenly a small fox face appeared under a hedge. It was Pablo!
The other cubs were so happy to see him again, they licked his
face all over. "Come and see what I've found," Pablo told them.

On the other side of the hedge was a beautiful wild park. At the center stood a shady tree.

Beneath its roots was a large sandy hole. A large, sandy EMPTY hole.

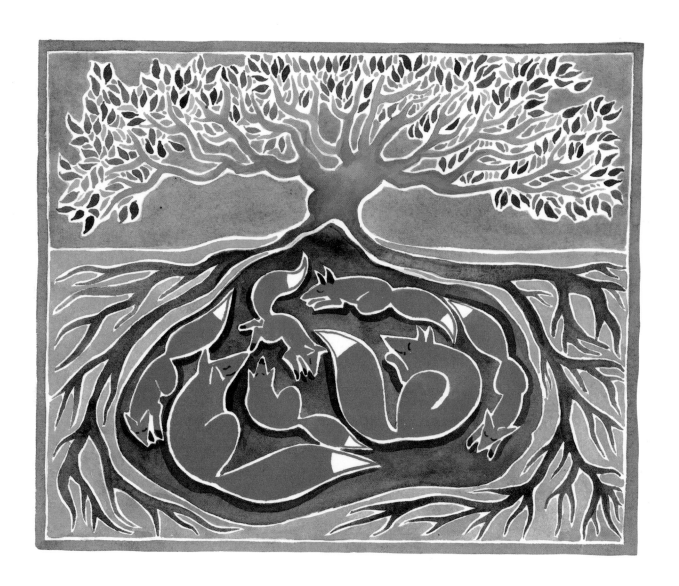

One by one they crept inside. There was just enough room for all of them.

Red Fox and his family had found their perfect new home at last.